Andrew's Own Place

Nancy Riecken   *Illustrated by Meg Kelleher Aubrey*

Houghton Mifflin Company
Boston 1993

Library of Congress Cataloging-in-Publication Data

Riecken, Nancy.
    Andrew's own place / Nancy Riecken : illustrated by Meg Kelleher
Aubrey.
        p.   cm.
    Summary: A young boy becomes worried when his daily routine is
upset by the family's trip to the woods.
    ISBN 0-395-64723-1
    [1. Security (Psychology)—Fiction.   2. Fear—Fiction.   3. Family
life—Fiction.]   I. Aubrey, Meg Kelleher, ill.   II. Title.
PZ7. R4276An   1993   92-22953
[E]—dc20   CIP
                        AC

Printed in the United States of America

WOZ   10   9   8   7   6   5   4   3   2   1

To my family—N.R.

For my sons Matthew and Michael—M.K.A.

When Andrew sat at the table, he had a red chair that only he could sit in. He sat between his mother and his big sister, Rachel, right where the table leg stuck out and hit his chair. He loved to eat oatmeal with raisins and brown sugar in his Vitamin Pals bowl. When Andrew ate oatmeal in his chair right where the table leg stuck out he was in a good place.

After he ate, Andrew used his own sparkley purple toothbrush. He had his own place to keep it in the third slot on the right on the toothbrush rack. Nobody ever tried to use his toothbrush or his slot. They were all his.

When Andrew went for a ride in the tan van, he even had his own seat, way in the back. He kept a special traveling toy there. It had tiny parts that fell apart. Mommy always dug them out of the seat and picked them up off the floor when he got home. Andrew kept a soft blue blanket on his seat, too, to rest on when he got tired of riding and looking and playing.

One morning when Andrew got up, his mother didn't make oatmeal. "What are we doing?" Andrew asked, rubbing his eyes as his sister Sarah helped him dress. She just said, "You'll see." By the time Rachel got him to the van, Andrew looked worried. "Don't be afraid, Andrew," she said. "We have a surprise!" Andrew's dad was at the van, but Mom wasn't anywhere. Andrew's face clouded up and his eyes felt misty.

Then Daddy lifted Andrew high and hugged him tight. "We're going hiking at the park, Andrew," he said. "And see—Mommy's coming right now."

"Good morning, honey!" Andrew's mother climbed into the van and gave him a big hug. "Sorry I'm late. I was getting our breakfast ready." Then Andrew felt happy. Now he could enjoy the ride.

Rides in the van were always fun. Andrew liked it when Daddy drove over high hills and made the van go bump, bump, bump over rough roads. The back of the van seemed to fly right off the road. Andrew pulled his blue blanket close around him. He felt the sunlight on his face and he heard the hummmmm of the van, and he felt he was in a very good place.

Before long, he saw big trees on both sides of the highway. "Here we are!" Dad said. Andrew looked at the woods. They were dark. The trees were thick. "Daddy, can we just watch the woods?" he asked. "Take my hand, Andrew, and we'll walk together," Daddy answered. Then Andrew let go of the van door and held his dad's hand tight.

They followed a narrow trail into the woods. Before long, the path led down a steep hill to a noisy stream. Mommy and Daddy both helped Andrew walk on the wet rocks across it. Then Mom said, "This looks like a good place for breakfast."

"Great!" exclaimed Rachel. "I thought you'd forgotten."

Mom opened the backpack and poured juice. Andrew drank his and waited patiently for his bowl of oatmeal. Sarah handed him a waxed paper package. "What's this?" Andrew asked, frowning at the package. "It's your breakfast," Sarah answered, biting into a cheese and egg sandwich.

"Mommy! Where's my oatmeal?"

"You have oatmeal bread in your sandwich," she replied smiling. "Try it, honey. You'll like it."

Andrew opened his sandwich and stared at it. "It's not oatmeal," he said, taking a little bite. "But . . . it's not bad."

As Andrew ate his sandwich, he looked around. "Is it safe out here?" he asked Sarah.

"Of course it's safe! All the wild animals live out here, and they're not scared. Why should you be?"

Andrew picked up his sandwich and moved over to Rachel. "Is it time to go home now?" He looked into her eyes.

Rachel's eyes met Andrew's. "Andrew, I love the woods! The birds are singing, you can see deer all over, and there are places to explore. Hiking is great!"

"I think I've seen enough of it," Andrew said, swallowing the last of his sandwich.

"Why don't we head upstream," Mom suggested, putting the paper trash into the backpack. They hiked along the stream until it led into a dark cave in the side of the hill.

"Let's explore!" said Sarah, and she started right in, but Dad stopped her. "Wait up, Sarah! Let me go first with a flashlight." Andrew saw Rachel take Daddy's hand as they went inside.

Andrew stared at the black hole before him and his toes seemed to dig right through his shoes into the path. His mouth went dry and his eyes filled with tears.

"I can't go in there!" he cried.

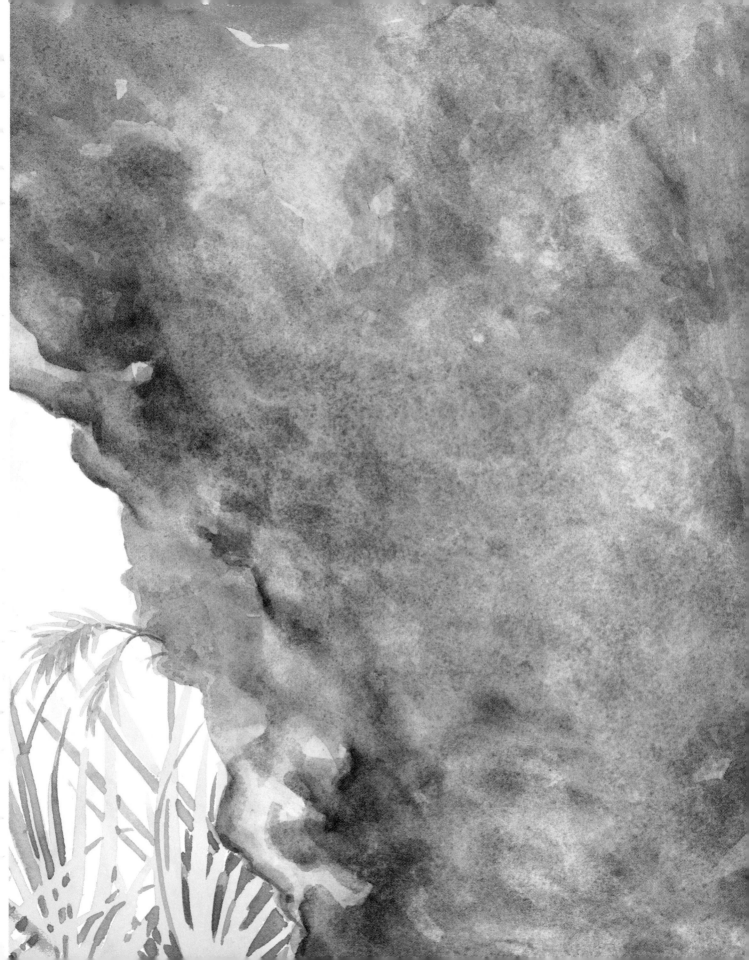

Mommy knelt down beside Andrew and hugged him. "It's safe, Andrew. I'm with you. Honey, we would never take you into a dangerous place." She patted his hand, and Andrew sighed, squeezed her hand tight, and stepped into the dark cave with her.

But even with Daddy's flashlight shining on the rocks, the cave looked big and scary. Andrew stopped and tugged on his mom's hand.

"Mommy, I just can't go in any more," he whispered, and hot tears ran down his cheeks.

"That's okay, Andrew. We'll wait outside," Mom said. They came back out. The sunlight sparkled on the splashing stream and the water danced over the rocks. Andrew thought he would rather follow it through the woods than listen to it gurgle in the black rocks of the cave.

"When will they come back?" he asked Mom after a while, peering back at the cave.

"Soon, honey."

Andrew watched the dark mouth of the cave. "Are they all right?"

"Yes, Andrew, they're fine. They're exploring the cave."

"Are you sure they're all right?"

"I'm sure."

Andrew listened to the silence of the cave. "Mommy?"

"Mmm?"

"Are there bears in that cave?"

"No, Andrew, there are no bears in the cave. Bears don't live around here."

Andrew sat and thought. "Mommy?"

"Yes, honey?"

"I think they need help."

"What do you want to do, Andrew?"

"Well," Andrew said, looking again at the dark cave, "I guess we'll have to go in there."

Mom watched as Andrew stood and took three slow steps toward the cave. Then he reached his hand out to her. They walked together back to the cave. Andrew peered inside and called, "Daddy? Sarah? Rachel!"

Suddenly Daddy's flashlight shone through the darkness. He and Sarah and Rachel followed it out into the sunshine. Andrew pulled on Sarah and Rachel's hands to make sure they were all right.

"You're okay, Daddy!" Andrew hugged him tight.

"I sure am, Andrew," Daddy replied, "and you're my big boy!"

Now the deep woods seemed pretty to Andrew. He danced along the edge of the stream and ran after Sarah and Rachel down the path.

Andrew soon discovered that walks in the woods could be tiring. After he had walked a long time, he slowed down. He stopped longer to look around. Finally, Mom picked him up and carried him. When she carried Andrew, he would wrap his arms around her neck and rest his head on her shoulder. He liked that. The sun glinted through the trees all around them. He was feeling warm and sleepy and very comfortable when Mom put him down.

"You get heavy, do you know that?" she asked him.

"Carry me," Andrew said, a little cross at having to stand up.

"I can't!" she sighed and looked at Daddy.

"Can you carry me?" Andrew asked his dad. "Mommy isn't carrying me at all."

"You don't think so?" Daddy asked with a smile. "Maybe you just don't remember."

Andrew nestled himself into Daddy's arms and rested his nose close behind Daddy's ear. "Well, I'd really like some oatmeal," he sighed.

"Are you hungry again?"

"Yes, I miss my oatmeal. I even miss my toothbrush." Andrew sighed a big, long sigh. "Daddy, I like the woods. But now I want to go home."

Dad carried Andrew all the way back to the van. Mom covered him with his soft blue blanket. Andrew barely felt the bump, bump, bump as he rode over the rough roads. When they glided over the hills, Andrew was sound asleep. But awake or asleep, with Mommy, Daddy, Sarah, and Rachel, Andrew knew he was in a very good place.